The
CAT
and the
KING

For Alison

First published in the UK in 2016 by Alison Green Books
An imprint of Scholastic Children's Books
Euston House, 24 Eversholt Street, London NW1 1DB
A division of Scholastic Ltd
www.scholastic.co.uk
London – New York – Toronto – Sydney – Auckland
Mexico City – New Delhi – Hong Kong

This edition published exclusively for Scholastic Book Clubs and Book Fairs

Copyright © 2016 Nick Sharratt

The portrait of the cat and the king on page 104 was drawn
by Ava Elise Morrice from Kingswells Primary School.
Reproduced by permission.

ISBN: 978 1 407 16691 9

The
CAT
and the
KING

Nick Sharratt

ALISON
GREEN
BOOKS

Chapter 1

Once upon a time there was a
king who lived in a rather grand
castle, with his best friend,
the cat.

The king was very good at doing all the things that kings do, like walking on red carpets, making speeches, cutting ribbons, and balancing a heavy crown on his head.

He had a dozen servants to do everything else.

Brring! Brring!

The cat was very good at making sure
everything ran smoothly in the castle.

He didn't say much, because cats don't actually talk, but he had nice, neat handwriting and a big supply of sticky notes on which he could write instructions.

Everything ticked along nicely in the castle – until an Unfortunate Incident that the cat could not prevent.

Let's just say it involved a fire-breathing dragon.

The Cat and the King

The Cat and the King

Fortunately no one was hurt, but the king and the cat had to move out of the castle and find somewhere else to live.

They looked at lots of places . . .

. . . and finally settled on Number 37, Castle Close, because the address had a nice, comforting ring to it.

Number 37 wasn't as grand as their previous home, but it didn't need to be, because now it was just the two of them, the cat and the king.

Right after the Unfortunate
Incident, the servants had
decided they didn't fancy
being servants any more
and had run off to find
other jobs.

15

And Number 37 didn't need to be grand because the king and the cat had next to no furniture left and hardly any possessions.

The king had his four-poster bed which, since the Unfortunate Incident, was now a three-poster bed.

He also had a trunk filled with bits and bobs (including his pyjamas and toothbrush),

and his crown (which he NEVER took off.)

The cat had his sticky notes,

his felt-tip pens,

his laptop,

his Swiss penknife

and the Royal Money Box.

He also had his driving licence, which meant they were able to hire a van to take themselves and what little they had to the new house.

The two of them stood outside the front door.
The king had never needed to open a door before
(there had always been a servant to do it for him)
and he wasn't sure how keys worked, either. So
the cat let them in – and that is how their life in
Castle Closc began.

Chapter 2

The next morning, the king and the cat were having a nice long lie-in after unpacking the van the night before.

It had been quite hard work for the king, because he wasn't used to lifting and carrying anything except sceptres and orbs and ceremonial swords.

It had been quite hard work for the cat, too.

The cat's bed had been destroyed in the Unfortunate Incident so, that first night, he and the king shared the three-poster bed, after the cat had reassembled it with the help of the screwdriver blade in his Swiss penknife.

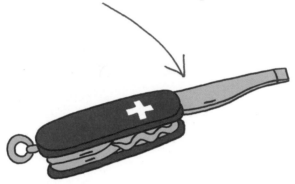

They were still dozing when the doorbell rang. The cat leapt out of bed and ran down to open the front door.

There on the doorstep were a friendly looking lady and two smiley children, a girl and a boy.

"Hello!" said the lady. "Welcome to Castle Close. We saw you moving in yesterday. We're your neighbours from Number 35. I'm Caroline and this is Cressida and Christopher. We're the Cromwells."

"We are in the
bedchamber!" boomed a
voice. "Hasten forth!"

The cat led everyone upstairs
and presented them to the king.

Mrs Cromwell and Cressida curtsied and Christopher burtsied. (A burtsey is a bow and a curtsey mixed together and Christopher had invented it.)

The king nodded, but said nothing.

"Welcome to Castle Close, Your Majesty," said Mrs Cromwell, and she handed the king a large round tin that had been decorated with glued-on paper crowns.

The king wasn't familiar with opening tins, and waited silently for the cat to take off the lid. Inside were golden-coloured, finger-shaped biscuits, dipped in chocolate.

"A house-warming present," said Mrs Cromwell.
"We made them ourselves," added Cressida.
"ROYAL Shortbread," announced
Christopher.
The king clapped his hands
and burst into a huge smile.

"Bravo!" he cried. "Bravo! We are most
pleased."

(He liked to say "we" instead of "I" when he
was addressing anyone other than the cat – it
was something kings did.)

The cat opened the trunk, rummaged around
and pulled out three gold medals.

Then, one by one, Mrs Cromwell, Cressida
and Christopher were solemnly
commanded by the king to step
forward and receive a special
honour each, for Services
to Baking.

Chapter 3

After the Cromwells had left, the king and the cat sat in the bed, nibbling fingers of Royal Shortbread. Even though the biscuits were delicious, the king looked a bit forlorn.

"I miss my hunting," he sighed.

Hunting was one of the "king things" that he'd liked doing most before the Unfortunate Incident. But it wasn't foxes or deer or boars or hares that the king had hunted.

It was thimbles.

On a hunting day, the cat would go out and hide a gold thimble in the grounds of the castle and the king would try to find it. It was much more fun than chasing wild animals.

It was much more of a challenge, too, because thimbles are so tiny, but the cat would provide a few clues to make it a bit easier.

Of course, all the thimbles had been lost in
the Unfortunate Incident, so there could be no
Hunt-the-Thimble this Sunday morning.

But the cat was a clever cat and had another
kind of hunting planned . . . Bargain Hunting!

The king and the cat got into the van and
drove to a car-boot sale on the outskirts of the
town where they now lived.

The aim of the Bargain Hunt was to buy all the things they needed for their new home without spending a huge amount of money. The king was very excited by this challenge, but he'd never actually bought anything before and had absolutely no idea about what things should cost, because the cat always dealt with that kind of thing.

Together they approached the first stall and looked hard at all the things on sale. The king saw something he liked, took a guess at what he should pay, and proclaimed in his special speech-making voice:

> We hereby, on this third Sunday in June, do make payment of one royal penny in exchange for one armchair.

The stallholder, who wasn't used to seeing kings at car-boot sales (or cats with money boxes, come to that) was so surprised that he just nodded his head and took the coin without saying a word.

The king and the cat moved on to the next stall and again examined everything closely. The cat pointed to a few items, the king had a ponder, and then declared:

We hereby, on this third Sunday in June, do make payment of one royal penny in exchange for one saucepan, one kettle and one mixing bowl.

34

The lady behind the stall, who never normally sold anything for less than 50p, was speechless. She opened her mouth but made no sound as the king pressed a little coin into her hand.

So it went on. By midday, the king and the cat had spent one single penny at each and every stall.

This is what they'd purchased:

an armchair,

a saucepan, a kettle
and a mixing bowl,

an artificial Christmas tree,

a laundry basket with
towels, tablecloths and
a feather boa inside it,

a beanbag,

an extendable
dining table and
two dining chairs,

a spice rack,

a mirror in the
shape of a butterfly,

a clock in the
shape of a dog,

a teapot in the
shape of a caravan,

a hammock,

a wheelbarrow,

a coffee table,

a tool box with
some tools in it,

a ceramic hen
to keep eggs in,

a filing cabinet full of
cutlery and crockery,

two deck chairs,

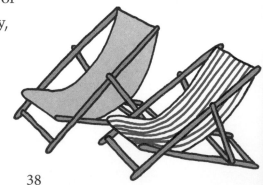

a cactus that
was also a lamp,

a lamp that
was also a globe,

a dictionary, a bumper book
of jokes and a book all
about making party cakes,

a set of giant
dominoes,

and a pirate-shaped
bottle of bubble bath.

They'd spent a grand total of twenty-two
pence.

Between them they loaded up the van (the king
felt he was really beginning to get the hang
of this lifting-and-carrying business)
and drove off, very pleased
with their purchases.

40

Later on, when the stallholders had finally recovered, they looked closely at their pennies and saw that they weren't just ordinary pennies. They were stamped with the king's head on one side and an image of the cat on the other, and they werc made of pure, solid gold.

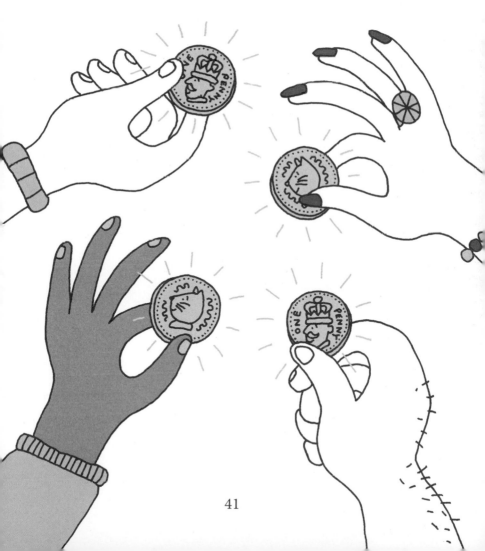

Chapter 4

On the way back home the cat and the king
stopped to buy some groceries.

It was the king's first time shopping in a
supermarket and he was delighted to find that
it was just another kind of jolly hunting game.
This time the hunt was for Food Fit for Royalty.
He ran ahead with a trolley, eagerly scanning the
shelves for the right things to buy.

By the time they reached
the check-out, the king
had tracked down:

frozen KING prawns,

Jersey ROYAL potatoes,

CORONATION
chicken sandwiches,

GOLDEN syrup,

GOLDEN Delicious apples,

two RUBY grapefruits,

ROYAL icing in
four different colours,

six KING-size bottles
of cola (on special offer),

a KING-size bag of
cheese-and-onion crisps

and a KING-size box of
assorted toffees and chocolates.

What feasts they would have
back at Number 37!

There was a lady in front of them at the check-out. The king had never queued before, and wasn't sure he liked it, but luckily he was distracted by the display of sweets. He added a tube of mint IMPERIALS to the shopping.

It was soon their turn. The cat paid and it was the king's job to pack.

"Do you need a bag?" asked the cashier (who looked vaguely familiar.)

Of course they didn't need a bag – they had the wheelbarrow.

Chapter 5

It was late afternoon. The king and the cat sat at the dining table, chewing toffees.

They'd been really busy, unloading the van, putting away the shopping, then sorting out where all the things from the car-boot sale should go.

They'd tried the furniture here,

and they'd tried the
furniture there.

The king was now an expert at lifting and
carrying and had been introduced to
pushing and pulling as well.

It was nearly four o'clock by the time they were able to have some lunch.

The king had never opened a pack of sandwiches before. He had tried and tried before giving up and handing it to the cat, who had struggled quite a bit, too. But, when the sandwiches were eventually freed, they had been delicious.

The toffees and chocolates were yummy as well, but the king was looking a little forlorn again.

"I miss my throne," he sighed, in between chews.

50

The king's throne had been a very fine
piece of furniture.

I'm sorry to report that it was damaged
beyond repair in the Unfortunate Incident.

They went into the living room and looked at the armchair and the beanbag on either side of the fireplace. The king wasn't interested in the beanbag, which was just as well, as the cat had picked that out for himself. The armchair did look quite comfy, but it really wasn't grand enough to be a throne.

The cat had a think.

He scrunched his shiny toffee-wrapper into a tight ball so that it looked like a precious stone.

He searched in the tool box, and pulled out a tube of extra-strong glue.

He dabbed some on the pretend jewel and stuck it firmly to one arm of the armchair.

"Bravo!" cried the king and, with great enthusiasm, he began scrunching up the wrappers that lay in a pile on the table. They worked as a team, the king scrunching and the cat dabbing and sticking.

They had to eat the rest of the toffees and chocolates to free up the wrappers.

An hour later, the chair was studded all over
with jewels and the job was almost done. The
cat fetched the feather boa from the laundry
basket and together they carefully positioned
it along the chair-back and glued it into place.
Then they stood back to admire their glittering,
sparkling, feathery handiwork.

The king, grinning from ear to ear, lowered himself gently into his magnificent new throne. He settled back with a sigh – only this time it was a sigh of happiness. The cat hopped on to his beanbag and nestled down.

Within minutes they'd both dozed off.

Chapter 6

The next day they needed to take the hire van
back. As they were motoring along, the cat could
see that the king was once again looking a bit
forlorn. The clever cat knew that the king was
thinking about his marching band and his Eleven
O'Clock Wave.

Every morning from Monday to Friday, at eleven o'clock precisely, the king would stand on the castle balcony and listen to his marching band as it paraded back and forth, playing one of his five favourite tunes. He never knew which tune it would be, so it was always a lovely surprise.

After that, the king would spend five minutes waving to the crowd that had come to watch him standing on his balcony. It gave the king a lot of pleasure to wave to the people as they cheered and waved back, and it was a bit of exercise for him, too.

The band was made up of six of the dozen servants who worked in the castle. At five-to-eleven the cat would blow a whistle, which was the signal for them to change out of their servant clothes, put on their band uniforms and pick up their instruments.

Now, I will let you in on a secret. It was also the signal for the other six servants to change out of their servant clothes, put on their everyday things and pretend to be the crowd that had come to see the king. However, the king didn't realise this, and the cat made sure that he never found out.

Once the hire van had been returned, the king and the cat went and stood at the bus stop. It was the king's second time in a queue, so he was still extremely new to waiting.

He tried to be patient like everyone else, but it was very, very, very difficult. He almost wept with joy when the bus finally arrived two-and-a-half minutes later.

The cat bought the tickets from the bus driver (who had a familiar look about her.) Then they clambered up to the top deck and found a seat right at the front.

As the bus set off, they heard a clock somewhere striking eleven. They might not have a marching band, but at least they were in a good place for the king to do some waving, which he now did most graciously to the passers-by on the pavement below.

It wasn't a great success:
not one person looked up and noticed.

The cat thought the king should try waving from the back seat, even if it meant twisting round quite a bit. Immediately behind their bus was another bus (and there was another bus behind that one, too, of course, because it's a fact that if you wait a long time for a bus, three will come along all at once.)

So the king was able to wave to his heart's content to the people sitting upstairs in the following bus – and they all smiled broadly and waved right back.

By the time they reached their stop the king was beaming with delight, even though his arm ached quite a lot and he had a stiff neck.

Chapter 7

The king and the cat settled into life at
Number 37.

The cat now had his own room and he was
very cosy in there. At eight o'clock in the
morning he would climb out of his hammock,
go downstairs, make two cups of tea and take
one up to the king in his bedchamber. (They
bought the tea bags and milk on their second
trip to the supermarket – to begin with they
drank cups of cola.)

The cat would then run the king a bath, because the king didn't know about turning taps on or off.

The cat prepared breakfast whilst the king was in the bath. I don't need to tell you that the king had never made breakfast, do I?
He had never even laid a table.

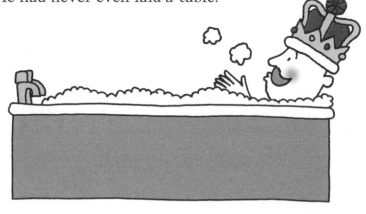

The king's favourite breakfast was a boiled egg and soldiers and, as luck would have it, that was the cat's favourite, too.

(The eggs and bread and butter were bought on the third trip to the supermarket – before that, they started the day with grapefruit halves, Royal Shortbread and apple slices dipped in golden syrup.)

After breakfast they did the dishes together because there was no way the cat was going to wash *and* dry. It was all very new for the king, but he did his best and gradually learned not to squeeze in so much washing-up liquid when it was his turn at the sink.

That done, they went to the bus stop. Each time the king got a tiny bit better at waiting, but it was most definitely not his favourite activity. When the three buses came together, they boarded the first one, went upstairs, headed for the back seat, and the king got on with waving, which made him very happy. The cat knew, however, that the king was still missing his marching band, and wished he could do something about it.

They hopped off at the supermarket to play
the hunting game, only the cat now chose what
to look for, and would give the king a neatly
written-out shopping list as soon as they entered
the store. They couldn't bring the wheelbarrow
on the bus, but they had found
some useful shopping
bags in a drawer in
the kitchen.

Now, there was another thing that the king missed about life at the castle. He missed riding his horses. They weren't real horses. The king found real horses a bit frightening, to be honest. The Royal Horses had been carved out of wood and painted bright colours, because the king had had his very own merry-go-round. How he had loved taking a spin on it!

And how quickly it had gone up in smoke during the Unfortunate Incident!

There weren't any horses at the supermarket, but there was an ostrich, a giant ladybird and a motorbike with a smiley face. If you put 50p in a slot, you could sit on them whilst they jiggled and swayed and lights flashed on and off.

So, as the prize for hunting down all the groceries on the shopping list, the cat would give the king money for a ride.

He had decided he liked the motorbike best because, unlike the ostrich and the ladybird, it made a good, throaty BRRRRRM-BRRRRM-BRRRRM noise.

(He liked the motorbike ride so much that he was even happy to wait his turn if there was a toddler on it before him.)

BRRRRRM!

BRRRRRM!

BRRRRRM!

The cat and the king didn't normally bother with the bus on the way home because, in actual fact, the supermarket was only just round the corner from where they lived.

Chapter 8

One Thursday, after they'd got back from shopping, the cat cooked lunch and the king had his first go at table-laying.

The cat rearranged the cutlery and they ate their meal of spaghetti and pesto sauce. Have you ever tried it? You should, because it's really tasty. It had been the cat's choice and, even though there wasn't anything royal in the name, the king loved it, too.

They had a Golden Delicious apple each for pudding,

and then it was joke time.

Back in the castle, the king's jester would come into the banqueting hall every day after lunch, to tell a joke. The jester was really one of the servants who, once the table had been cleared, would quickly put on the jester's costume and try to think of a new joke fit for a king.

Some of his efforts were better than others. See what you think:

> When is a piece of wood like a king?
> *When it's a ruler.*

> What does a king wear when it's wet outside?
> *A reign coat.*

> Where does a king keep his armies?
> *Up his sleevies.*

> What is a king's favourite monster?
> *King Kong.*

> What is a king's favourite car?
> *A Royals Royce.*

> Which is a king's favourite American state?
> *Kingtucky.*

If the king didn't find the joke funny, he would proclaim grandly: "We are NOT amused!" But as he thoroughly enjoyed saying those four words, he always liked joke time, whether the jester's joke was good or bad.

They didn't have a jester any more, but they did have the bumper book of jokes from the car-boot sale.

The king closed his eyes and chose the joke for the day by opening the pages at random and stabbing with his finger. Today's joke had nothing to do with kings. It was a cat joke.

"*What did the cat have for breakfast?*" read the king. "*Mice Crispies.*" He thought for a while, then proclaimed with great satisfaction, "We are NOT amused!"

The cat, on the other hand, found the joke utterly hilarious and couldn't stop chuckling for ages.

Then, as it was such a lovely, sunny afternoon, the pair of them went and sat outside in the deck chairs. Once the cat had finally got over the joke, he saw that the king's forlorn expression had returned.

"I miss my banquets," he sighed.

Back in the old days, another one of his favourite "king things" had been to hold a Royal Banquet. The servants would prepare a magnificent feast and bring all the dishes out under huge silver domes, to be placed on the long table in the Banqueting Hall.

Important guests would then arrive from far and wide. There would always be twelve of them, dressed very smartly.

The truth of the matter was that these guests were the king's dozen servants, having changed into their party clothes but, once again, the king didn't realise this. And, once again, the cat made sure he never found out.

The servants, by the way, didn't mind this part of their job one little bit, because they got to eat all the wonderful food they'd made and have a nice, relaxing afternoon. It put them in a very good mood and they were quite happy to listen politely when the time came for the king's speech, and to clap and cheer him when it was over.

The king was remembering those jolly
occasions as he lay in his deck chair. The cat
saw him wipe away a tear and felt sorry for him.
He wondered what to do – they couldn't have a
Royal Banquet at Number 37 because they didn't
have a banqueting hall, but . . . but . . . but . . .
they could have a Royal Garden Party instead!
And they could invite the Cromwells, the nice
family from next door.

The cat fetched his felt-tip pens and a handy sheet of card. He drew a smart decorative border and, within it, in his best writing, he wrote:

I, the cat,
am commanded by the King
to invite you to a
Royal Garden Party

at three o'clock on Saturday afternoon

Morning Dress for the gentlemen
Hats for the ladies

R.S.V.P.

"Bravo!" cried the king, when the cat showed him the invitation. He picked up a pen and added:

Do you like the way he underlined his signature? Signing things was one of the "king things" he was particularly good at.

By the way, you might be wondering what the king's real name was. It was:

Theodore
Hadrian
Engelbert
Kensington
Isambard
Nicholai
Gideon.

But that was far too much to say or write, so he took the first letter of each name, and that made:

THE KING.

Perhaps you're also wondering what the cat was called. His name was Tibbles, but he much preferred to be known as "the cat".

The cat immediately took the finished
invitation round to Number 35 and popped
it through the letterbox.

Then the king and the cat spent the rest of
the afternoon planning the garden party.

Chapter 9

Cressida and Christopher Cromwell were very excited when they found the invitation lying on the doormat – as was Mrs Cromwell when she came home from work.

They chatted away over the dinner table, discussing what they would wear for the occasion.

Mr Cromwell, on the other hand, sat there with his arms folded, looking grumpy and humpfing quite a lot.

"Load of nonsense," he said. "I'm not going to bow, curtsey or burtsey to a neighbour. I'm not going to call him 'Your Majesty' and I'm *not* going to get togged up in morning dress, either."

"Will *I* have to get a morning dress?" asked Christopher, thinking it sounded an odd thing for a boy to have to wear, especially in the afternoon.

"I'm sure your favourite shirt will be just fine. With a tie, perhaps, and your medal, of course," Mrs Cromwell replied.

She looked at her husband. "As for you, Ollie, you can wear whatever you like, so long as it's not your tracksuit."

Mr Cromwell humpfed.

Humpf!

"What do you think we'll get to eat and drink?" wondered Cressida.

"Humpf!" went Mr Cromwell. "You know what kings eat, don't you? Boars' heads and roasted swans and larks' tongues. Poor little birds."

Both the children shrieked in disgust.

Mrs Cromwell told her husband to stop being so naughty.

Christopher picked up the invitation again. "What does 'R.S.V.P.' mean?" he asked.

"It means we must send a nice reply," said his mum. "So you, Ollie, can drop a note round right now saying we'd be delighted to come."

Mr Cromwell frowned and made an extra-loud "*humpf*" noise.

Humpf!

He was still humpfing on Saturday morning as he stood at the bathroom mirror, shaving. But then he happened to glance out of the window into next door's garden, and saw the king and the cat bringing out a set of giant dominoes.

Mr Cromwell's eyes lit up. The thought that there might be games to play that afternoon cheered him up enormously.

Chapter 10

At three o'clock on the dot, the doorbell of Number 37 rang. The cat opened the door and greeted the Cromwells. As you know, the cat wasn't one for talking, but he smiled politely and shook everyone's hand.

The Cromwells had really made an effort with their outfits, and Mrs Cromwell and the children proudly sported their gold medals.

Mr Cromwell was wearing a dinner jacket with a flower in the lapel and a polka-dot bow tie. But, if you looked closely, you could see that the jacket, flower and tie were actually printed on a t-shirt. He was also wearing shorts instead of long trousers.

The cat led them through to the back garden, which the king and cat had set out like a banqueting hall. The dining table had been brought outside and around it stood the dining chairs, deck chairs, beanbag and, in central position, the throne, upon which sat the king. He and the cat had carried out all the furniture that morning (actually, the king had done most of the carrying.)

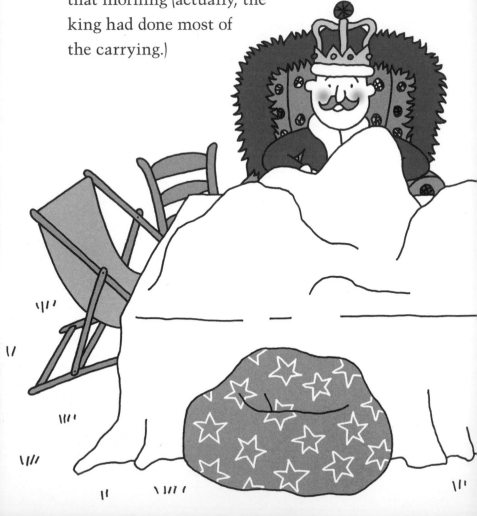

The table was covered in a large white sheet, beneath which were some intriguing lumps and bumps.

The king smiled at the guests. "We bid you welcome," he said.

Two Cromwells curtsied, one Cromwell burtsied and one Cromwell made a loud *"humpf!"* sound.

The King gestured to the chairs and everyone took a seat. "Let the feasting begin!" he cried, with a clap of his hands, and the cat whipped away the sheet.

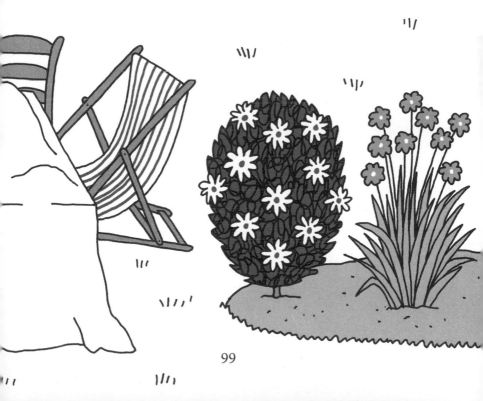

99

The Cromwells' jaws all dropped open at
once. They stared in silent horror at a huge
boar's head with an apple gripped in its jaws; a
great big swan, still covered in white feathers,
and an enormous pie with a pastry crust out
of which poked lots of blackbirds' heads, their
orange beaks pointing at the sky.

"Tuck in! Tuck in!" encouraged the king,
and he leaned forward and snapped the head off
the swan. The two children and Mr Cromwell
all squealed but, strangely, Mrs Cromwell now
looked rather amused. She reached over, chopped
off one of the boar's tusks with her knife and put
it on Christopher's plate.

"Cake," she chuckled. "They're all made out of cake!"

She was right. The day before, the king and the cat had made three magnificent cakes, following recipes they'd found in the party-cake book. To be honest, the cat had done most of the baking and decorating (he was a *very* clever cat) but the king had helped lick out the bowls and had washed AND dried all the pots and pans.

The boar's head was
really chocolate gâteau;

the swan was
vanilla sponge,

and the blackbird
pie was coffee-
and-walnut cake.
Yummy!

They all piled their plates high. Even Mr
Cromwell had to admit the cakes tasted
absolutely amazing. The adults drank cups of
tea and the children drank cups of cola.

When they'd all eaten their fill, Christopher stood up, burtsied and presented a scroll of paper to the king.

"I've drawn you a picture, Your Majesty," he announced proudly.

The king unrolled the paper and gasped in delight when he saw a very fine double portrait of himself and the cat, both looking most handsome.

The cat smiled appreciatively, too, and thought how well the picture would look over the fireplace.

"Bravo, bravo! You are truly talented, young man. We thank you most kindly," said the king with feeling and, in the wink of an eye, the cat had dashed inside the house and returned with a gold medal for Services to Art.

Next, Cressida stepped forward and curtsied.
"I would like to play for you, Your Majesty,"
she declared, and lifted a recorder to her lips,
whilst Mr Cromwell held up her music book.

When he heard the melody, the king couldn't
have been happier – *Hot Cross Buns* was one of
his five favourite tunes!

Cressida played
beautifully, with hardly
any mistakes. When she'd
finished, she got a loud
round of applause.

"Splendid, splendid! Bravo! Bravo! Bravo!" cheered the king. "What else is in your repertoire?"

"I know *London's Burning, Yankee Doodle* and *Frère Jacques* and I'm just learning the *James Bond* theme tune," said Cressida.

The king nearly burst with excitement – by some extraordinary miracle they were the remaining four of his five favourite tunes.

"Perhaps Cressida could pop by with her dad after school and play one of the pieces for you when she does her daily recorder practice," suggested Mrs Cromwell, after her daughter had received a medal for Services to Music. "And Christopher could bring along his tambourine."

Mr Cromwell was about to humpf loudly, but it did occur to him that there might be more scrumptious cake on offer if he and the children were to visit again, so he kept quiet. The king was overjoyed because it would be just like having his marching band once more. And the cat was overjoyed for the king.

After tea, they all paired
up to play giant dominoes.
They played three rounds and
each time the children won.

They jumped up
and down gleefully.

The king cheered, "Huzzah!" and the cat and Mrs Cromwell clapped.

Mr Cromwell tried very, very, very hard not to start humpfing. He loved playing games but he very much liked to win.

So he was very excited when the king declared that they would play a ball game next, even though it wasn't one he'd ever played before.

The game had the fancy name of "Bilboquet" (which the king pronounced as "Bilb-okay".) It was a catching game, involving a cup with a ball attached to it by a piece of string.

Everyone was allowed a bit of a practice. Then the contest was on to see who could catch the ball in the cup the most times in a row. The king went first.

He was a lot more used to the game
than the rest of them, of course,
and caught the ball twelve
times in a row.

Cressida managed three
times, Christopher managed
five,

Mrs Cromwell
managed six

and the cat managed none
(he was good at lots of things,
but not Bilboquet.)

Then it was Mr Cromwell's go. He pulled himself up straight, stood with his feet planted firmly on the ground and took a few deep breaths. Then he began.

He got past three catches;

he got past
five catches;

he got past six

and he got past twelve.
Mr Cromwell was
a natural!

When the ball finally missed the cup he had
managed a grand total of one-hundred-and-forty-
six non-stop catches.

Everyone clapped and cheered, and cheered and clapped. The king congratulated Mr Cromwell warmly and awarded him a gold medal for Outstanding Sporting Achievement. Mr Cromwell beamed with pride. He decided it wasn't so bad having a king live next door after all.

The king felt it was time to make a speech. He was just about to begin when something went . . .

Chapter 11

On top of the garden shed crouched a dragon.
It was bright red and the size of a small car.
It stared menacingly at them with narrowed
fluorescent-green eyes, and blew two puffs of
nasty-smelling smoke from its nostrils.

"Cor!" squeaked Christopher. "That's an AMAZING cake!"

But it wasn't a cake . . . it really was a real dragon.

The king started shaking all over and the cat's fur stood right up on end. It was the very same dragon that had caused the Unfortunate Incident at the beginning of the story.

Let me tell you a little more about this particular dragon. It was the fire-breathing kind, obviously. In order to keep the flames in its tummy from going out, it never drank water and avoided nearly all liquids except for:

cooking oil,

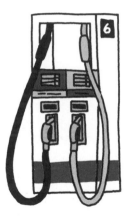

white spirit,

petrol

and the occasional
bottle of nail polish.

It was very greedy but, thankfully, it wasn't wild about eating humans or cats, because they didn't taste smoky enough.

What it really liked were foods such as:

smoked ham,

smoked cheese,

smoked fish

and smoky-bacon-
flavoured crisps,

all of which, it has to be said, can be rather
delicious. If only there had been something
smoky-tasting that day at the castle, the
Unfortunate Incident would never have
happened.

Right now, the dragon was in the mood
for a snack, but it couldn't see anything
good to eat. (There was a little bit of
cake left, but the dragon didn't
have a sweet tooth.)

When the dragon was hungry it became tetchy, and a tetchy dragon is not ideal, because things tend to get burnt down. It gave another deafening roar,

RAAAARGH!!!

and a huge flame shot out of its mouth, which sent everyone scurrying back to the house.

They stared, horrified, as the dragon slid off the shed roof and began to lumber towards them. It twisted its head from side to side as it went, kicking dominoes out of its path and blowtorching the odd shrub to a blackened crisp with a burst of its fiery breath.

If someone didn't act fast, there was going to be another Unfortunate Incident! But the poor king was too upset even to speak, as was the cat (had it been the speaking kind.)

Mr and Mrs Cromwell decided to take
charge. They looked around for ammunition and
saw that there were four unopened king-size
bottles of cola standing next to the fridge. Mrs
Cromwell grabbed a bottle, shook it for all she
was worth, and tossed it to Mr Cromwell.

He loosened the cap
with a hiss and hurled the
bottle into the back garden.

It hit the ground just in front of the dragon
and a king-size quantity of super-fizzy cola
exploded every which way, soaking the
startled animal from snout to tail.

The dragon gasped, only to end up with a
great big mouthful of bubbles as a second bottle
crash-landed at its feet. Two more bottles flew
through the air, spewing sugary drink and
drenching the bewildered beast with froth.

It spluttered helplessly as cola trickled out
of its nose and dripped from its scales. The
question was: had it swallowed enough to put
out the flames in its stomach?

They watched tensely through the window as the soggy creature recovered itself, reared up, spread its claws and thumped the ground with its heavy tail. It glared at them with a look of evil triumph and stretched its mighty jaws wide apart.

They braced themselves for a scorching blast of fire. But all that came out was an extremely loud

BURP!

Deeply embarrassed, the dragon unfurled its sticky wings and hurriedly flew away, hoping it might find another dragon somewhere with a box of matches.

Chapter 12

An enormous cheer burst from the kitchen.

Back into the garden ran the king, the cat and the Cromwells.

The king immediately awarded Mr and Mrs Cromwell medals for Bravery and Resourcefulness in a Time of Crisis, and Cressida and Christopher gazed with wonder and pride at their heroic parents.

The king made his speech. He thanked his guests for coming and for being the most splendid neighbours.

He and the cat would be forever grateful to Mr and Mrs Cromwell for preventing a disaster with their quick-thinking actions.

He looked forward greatly to gifted Cressida's recorder recitals.

He considered Christopher's picture a masterpiece, and promised it would hang in pride of place at Number 37.

Then he turned to the cat.

"And what would have become of me, my dear friend, if it weren't for you?" he asked. "You are the best companion this king could ask for, and I would be well and truly lost without you. Thank you from the bottom of my heart."

The king's speech made the cat far happier than any medal could have done. (He wouldn't have wanted one pinned to his fur in any case.)

Everyone agreed it had been a truly wonderful garden party, which even an unwelcome visit from a dragon hadn't been able to spoil.

After they'd waved the Cromwells off home, the king and the cat cleared the table and carried the furniture back inside.

They toured the garden to make sure there weren't any still-smouldering shrubs anywhere. Then, exhausted, they went indoors. The afternoon had been such a success, they were both eager to plan lots more royal activities, and the cat popped up to his bedroom to fetch his laptop.

But by the time he returned, the king had
drifted off to sleep in his throne. So the cat
settled down on his beanbag as quietly as he
could. He curled himself up into a comfy ball
and purred

and purred

and purred.

A Recipe for Royal Shortbread

Always ask an adult to help you
when you're cooking.

✳ ✳ ✳   Ingredients: ✳ ✳ ✳

175g butter at room temperature

90g caster sugar

210g plain flour

50g cornflour or semolina

150g chocolate (plain,

milk or white)

✳ ✳ ✳   Here's what you do: ✳ ✳ ✳

Pre-heat the oven to 170°C/325°F/Gas 3

• In a big bowl, beat the
butter with a wooden
spoon or electric mixer
until it's pale and creamy.

- Add the sugar, a bit at a time, and beat till it's fluffy and light in colour.

- Sieve the flour and cornflour (or semolina) into the butter mixture.

- Stir lightly, then use your hands (make sure they're nice and clean!) to bring the mixture gently together into a soft dough. Try not to handle it too much, or your shortbread will be a bit tough.

- With a rolling pin, roll the dough out on to a clean, flat surface, until it's about 1cm thick. Then cut it into fingers (you should get about 12.)

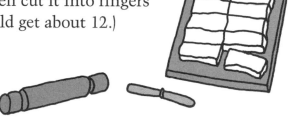

- Line a baking sheet with baking parchment, and carefully space the shortbread fingers out on it.

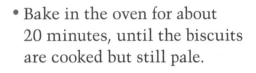

- Bake in the oven for about 20 minutes, until the biscuits are cooked but still pale.

- Let them cool on the tray till they firm up a bit, then transfer them to a wire rack to get completely cold.

✳ ✳   To make your shortbread   ✳ ✳
Royal, dip one end in chocolate:

- You'll need a sheet of baking parchment, big enough to lay all of the biscuits on, with a bit of space between them.

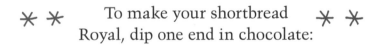

- Put a couple of centimetres of water in a small saucepan.

- Break the chocolate into small pieces and put them in a heat-proof bowl. Sit the bowl in the saucepan. The bowl mustn't touch the water, or the chocolate will burn.

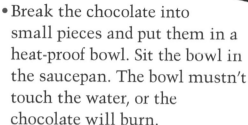

- Heat the water and let it simmer gently, till the chocolate has melted.

- Dip one end of the biscuits in the chocolate, then lay them on the baking parchment to dry.

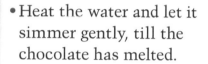

* *      * *

Fit for a king (or queen or prince or princess!)